Hands & Hearts

By
DONNA JO NAPOLI

Illustrated by
AMY BATES

ABRAMS BOOKS FOR YOUNG READERS · NEW YORK

The illustrations in this book were created using pencil and watercolor.

Library of Congress Cataloging-in-Publication Data

Napoli, Donna Jo, 1948–
Hands and hearts / by Donna Jo Napoli.
pages cm
Summary: "Highlights the bond between a mother and her
child while providing a gentle introduction to sign language
during their day at the beach"—Provided by publisher.
Includes bibliographical references.
ISBN 978-1-4197-1022-3
[1. Hand—Fiction. 2. Sign language—Fiction. 3. Beaches—
Fiction. 4. Mother and child—Fiction.] I. Title.
PZ7.N15Hal 2014
[E]—dc23
2013022194

Text copyright © 2014 Donna Jo Napoli
Illustrations copyright © 2014 Amy Bates
Book design by Maria T. Middleton

Printed and bound in China
10 9 8 7 6 5 4 3 2 1

Abrams Books for Young Readers are available at special discounts when purchased
in quantity for premiums and promotions as well as fundraising or educational
use. Special editions can also be created to specification. For details, contact
specialsales@abramsbooks.com or the address below.

ABRAMS
THE ART OF BOOKS SINCE 1949
115 West 18th Street
New York, NY 10011
www.abramsbooks.com

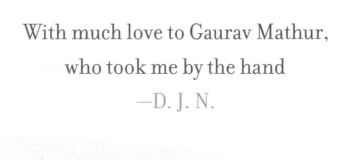

With much love to Gaurav Mathur,
who took me by the hand
—D. J. N.

For Halle, Jade, Macy, Wee-wee, Elsie,
Maddie-loo, Iris, and Jax
—A. B.

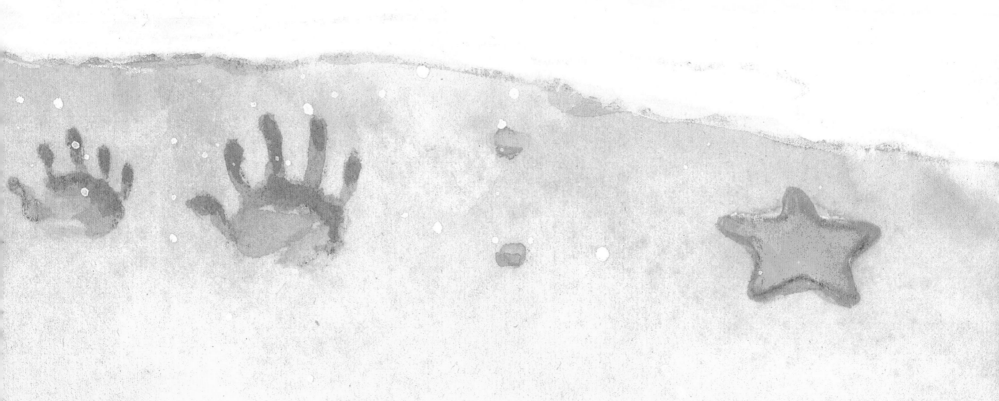

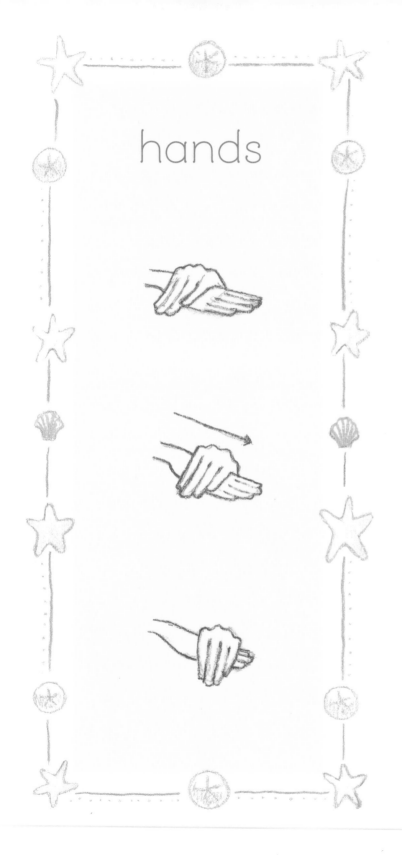

hands

My small hands
pull your big hands
tug and lug
till you're on your feet

Yak yak hands
yak yak fingers
telling as we run
out the gate down the path

run

flowers

Funny hands
funny fingers
flutter on the flowers
point at the gulls

Take my hands
and dance me dizzy
swing me around
fly me to the dunes

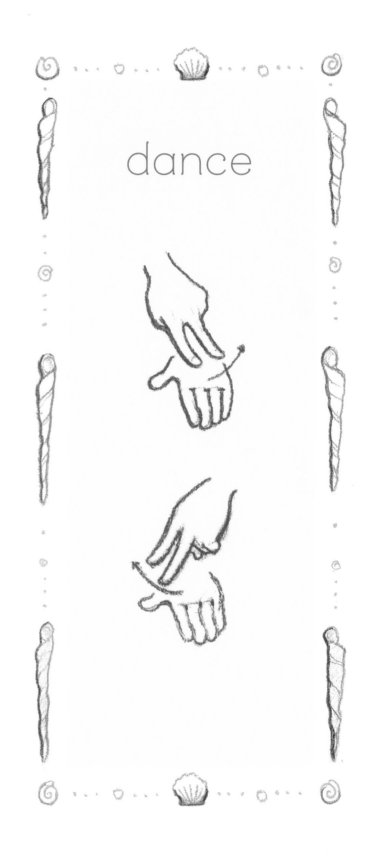

dance

hello

Flapping to the beach
hello to the waves
spraying and splashing
shoes left behind

Take my arms
and hold on tight
roll me in the sand
dip me in the sea

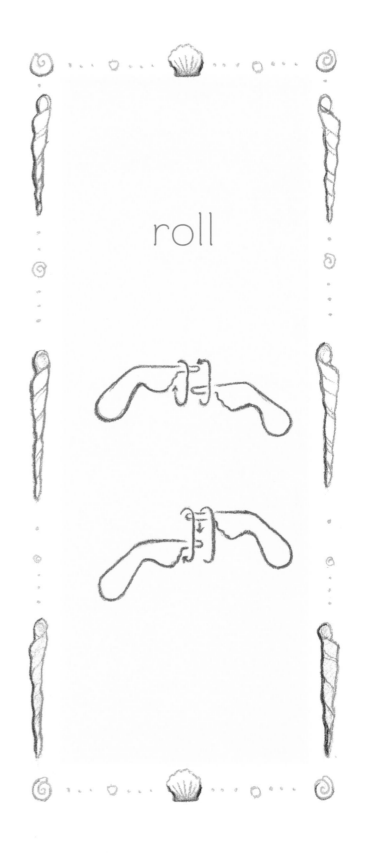

roll

swim

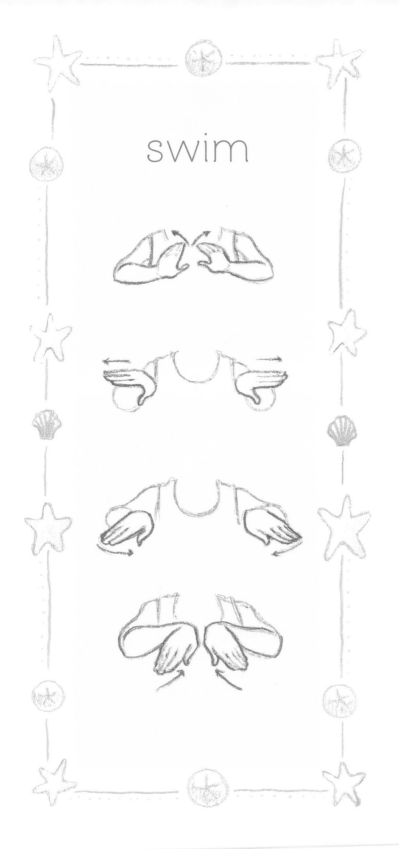

Let go hands
let go fingers
swim and glide
and reach for the raft

Dig a tunnel
dig a moat
dump in water
fill it full

water

wall

Build a tower
shape a wall
press on shells
to make it shine

Bury our toes
bury our knees
leaning lazy
small on tall

small

tall

sun

Make a tent
to hide from the sun
a spot to rest
and cuddle cozy

Hands to hold
hands to play
hands to yak
and kiss tips as we laugh

sunset

Watch the day
come to a close
sunset, sunset
glowing rosy

Wave to the whitecaps
wave to the gulls
bye-bye, bye-bye
home we go

Dear Reader,

I have been learning about deaf cultures and about sign languages for twenty years. Sign languages are different all around the world. But in all of them you can express anything you want, just as in a spoken language, only you use your hands and face to do it. A small change in hand-shape or movement of the arm and hand, for example, can give a different message—sometimes entirely different, sometimes only slightly different. This means that children who sign can express subtle distinctions that in a spoken language might call for specialized or grown-up vocabulary. I love that about sign languages. They give children expressive power at a very young age.

I hope this book will make you want to explore being expressive with your hands and face. Knowing a sign language is wonderful, whether you are deaf or hearing. If you want a peek at some American Sign Language signs, I recommend the online dictionary at http://www.aslpro.com/cgi-bin/aslpro/aslpro.cgi. If you want to learn how to use American Sign Language, try contacting a local community college or deaf-and-hearing communication center, as they often have classes for children, for adults, and for families.

My own work on sign languages is of three sorts. First, I am a linguist and I analyze the structure of languages. Second, I am an activist and I work for the language rights of deaf children. Third, I am a writer and I write books that aim to help deaf children learn to read and books that include deaf characters. You can find out more about my linguistic and activist writings at http://www.swarthmore.edu/SocSci/Linguistics/xling12napoli.html. And you can find out more about my fiction writings at http://www.donnajonapoli.com.

Love,
Donna Jo Napoli